our
generation®

This is Shannon's story.

SHANNON™

MAGIC UNDER
THE STARS

BY

SUSAN CAPPADONIA LOVE

ILLUSTRATED BY TRISH ROUELLE

An Our Generation® *book*

MAISON JOSEPH BATTAT LTD. *Publisher*

A very special thanks to the editor,
Joanne Burke Casey.

Our Generation® Books is a registered trademark of Maison Joseph Battat Ltd.
Text copyright © 2012 by Susan Love

ISBN: 978-0-9883165-3-9
Printed in China

For Ellen,
the queen of road trip fun.

Read all the adventures in the
Our Generation® Book Series

Read more about **Our Generation®** books and dolls online:
www.ogdolls.com

CONTENTS

EXTRA! EXTRA! READ ALL ABOUT IT!
*Big words, wacky words, powerful words, funny words...
what do they all mean? They are marked with this symbol *.
Look them up in the Glossary at the end of this book.*

Chapter One

NOWHERE TO HIDE

Two words changed my life forever. You might think they'd be two important words like "Help Me!" or "I'm Sorry!" or "Dream Big!" Or perhaps "Happy Birthday!", "Free Candy!" or "You Won!"

No, the two words that changed everything for me just suddenly appeared at the bottom of the list I'd made: Things to Bring on My Cross-Country* Camping Adventure!!!

All of the words were hand written in pencil, except for the last two, which were done in blue ink in my mom's neat writing.

I'd made the list for our dream vacation that was just a few days away. It was a scavenger hunt that would begin at our home in Boston, Massachusetts, and continue across the entire United States as we drove all the way to California.

Just me (Shannon), my mom, my dad and my dog (Luckie)—all together on a three-week camping trip! How fun!

The list was on the bedroom floor next to me where I had been snoozing in my sleeping bag. It was the first thing I reached for when I woke up.

My mom must have added this two-word item after I'd fallen asleep the night before. It was the only item that hadn't been packed and crossed out.

And those two words were something that I definitely had not planned on bringing along for the ride.

THINGS TO BRING ON MY
Cross-Country Camping Adventure!!!

~~travel journal~~	~~backpack~~
~~swimsuit~~	~~sunscreen~~
~~batteries~~	~~flip-flops~~
~~rain jacket~~	~~toothbrush~~
~~binoculars~~	~~hiking boots~~
~~playing cards~~	~~books~~
~~lantern~~	~~bug spray~~
~~Luckie's ball~~	~~sunglasses~~
~~Luckie's water bowl~~	~~tent~~
~~flashlight~~	your cousin

Your cousin? I felt confused. Were we bringing my cousin, Neve, on our family vacation?!

My cousin, who was snoozing in *my* bed at that very moment because she said sleeping bags are too hot and uncomfortable? Who joked that bags are for potato chips and not for people to sleep in?

My cousin, who had been visiting us from San Francisco, California, with her mom and dad, and who was already homesick after just three days?

My cousin, who shrieks if she even *thinks* she sees a spider? (And that's when it's on the *outside* of the window!)

My cousin, who would rather be inside reading a book about a mountain than climbing one?

Neve did not seem ready for the great outdoors—and I'm not sure the great outdoors was ready for Neve.

I wriggled deeper in my sleeping bag and stewed*. I clutched the list tightly in my fist and thought about this disappointing situation.

Let's be honest, I said to myself, *am I really feeling this way because Neve isn't the outdoorsy type like me?* Sort of. But that wasn't the whole story.

Neve and I were born on the same day, but that is the only way we're alike. Since we were toddlers, we've always been like oil and water, which is to say we don't mix. It seems like we just can't agree on *anything*.

I'm crazy about dogs. Neve not so much—she adores cats. I'm a huge fan of the Boston Red Sox baseball team. Neve roots for the San Francisco Giants.

We can't even agree on the best way to

toast a marshmallow. I cook mine until it's burnt on the outside and so gooey on the inside it practically melts off the stick. Neve prefers them just lightly golden brown and only a bit warm on the inside.

We're complete opposites! We even *live* on opposite sides of the United States.

I had vowed to myself that I would try to get along with Neve while she was here. She was visiting for only five days, so I knew that I could make the best of it.

But now we'll be trapped in the backseat together for three weeks! I thought. *I wish I could use my pink eraser and make those two words disappear.*

Also, I had this picture in my mind for months. My "Big Plan." My family hitting the open road in the pink, 4x4* car that we'd rented. Luckie right beside me. Hiking and campfires and adventures ahead.

We were towing a silver RV, which stands for recreation vehicle. It's the coolest travel trailer ever, with pink-and-white patterned curtains and pillows, stools, a sleeping area, stove and mini fridge.

It was my dream come true—well, *almost*—if my amazing travel plans hadn't suddenly taken this seriously wrong turn.

Chapter Two

TWO (UN)HAPPY CAMPERS

"C-camping?!" Neve choked on a bite of her waffle that morning when her mother told her the plan. She thumped her chest with her hand and coughed.

"You mean, like outdoors?" she squeaked. "Where there's poison ivy and bugs and scary animal noises at night and...." Her elbows rested on the table and her hands smooshed her cheeks together.

My dad looked from Neve's frown to mine. "Speaking of bugs, what does the mama firefly say to the baby firefly every night?"

"You're the light of my life," Neve muttered*.

I added the rest of the punch line*, "and we really must get glowing now."

My dad is an entomologist (that's a scientist who studies insects). He knows and loves every bug joke ever told. Neve and I have heard them all. We looked at each other and shook our heads.

"Listen, Neve," my Uncle Bo said, "you and Shannon live so far away from each other since we moved last year. This is a wonderful chance to spend time together."

Aunt Nellie put her arm around Neve's shoulders. "You love history and geography. Now you can actually see all those places you've read about."

"And check this out," my mom said. She hauled the Backseat Fun Basket she'd put together onto the dining room table. It was stuffed with large white envelopes.

She pointed to a number written on the top of each. "There's one for every day of the trip. They're filled with activities and games to keep the drive fun. Some contain a scavenger hunt clue to tell us what our next destination* will be."

Uncle Bo clapped his hands together. "I don't know why it took us so long to come up with it. This 'cousins' trip is such a great idea."

Neve and I glanced* at one another. Great idea?! At last we actually agreed on something. This was *not* such a great idea.

❧ ☙

For starters, we began squabbling* before we even got to the 4x4 car. We both "called" the left side of the backseat at the same time. To settle the matter, we flipped a coin and Neve won.

Right away Neve "moved in" and arranged her things on "her" side: a large, fluffy pillow, a bag of snacks, her lucky penny, an extra-large picture of her best friend, Cynthia (who she said is the coolest, nicest person ever), 7 books, 4 tubes of poison ivy cream, 3 cans of bug spray and 5 of her favorite stuffed animals. The pile spilled in every direction.

It looked pretty crowded, even though no one was sitting in the backseat yet.

My Aunt Nellie tried to sound positive. "Well, it will certainly be cozy back there."

To top it off, Luckie gave Neve about 20 slobbery kisses, which seemed to annoy her. It was his way of saying he was thrilled she was coming along.

Later on, my dad gave Neve and me our

own travel guidebooks and maps of the United States. He drew an invisible line with his finger on a map to show us which states we'd pass through. That way we could follow our route from state to state.

He was careful not to give away exactly where in each state we'd go. That would make the clues for the scavenger hunt too easy to figure out.

"Go through your travel guidebooks," my dad said, "and find one special place that you'd each like to visit. Put this ladybug sticker where it's located on your map."

"Does Luckie get to pick a special place, too?" I teased.

"Sure," Dad said. "I'll leave it up to you girls to pick one for Luckie."

Neve pointed to a page in her travel guidebook. "How about the No More Kisses Café?"

I couldn't help but giggle.

My dad laughed, too. "Make your

selections by tomorrow afternoon so we can plan those stops into our vacation."

The day before our big trip, Neve said a tearful goodbye to her mom and dad at the airport.

Aunt Nellie said she couldn't wait to hear all the stories Neve would come home with. Uncle Bo gave Neve a sheet of stamps so she could send postcards from the places we visited.

Neve was quiet on the ride home, then read the travel guidebook from cover to cover all afternoon.

Since she did not seem like she was in the mood to play, I decided to look through my travel guidebook, too. There are so many interesting places, it was difficult to pick just one.

I finally put my ladybug sticker on Fresno, California. There was a tour there that I just had to go on.

That night, my mom called a family meeting to discuss last-minute details. Did we all pack our pajamas and pillows? Check. A tarp to put under the tent in case of rain? Check. The safety kit? No one had, so my mom put us on that job.

Neve seemed to brighten up, helping me collect a few items that were missing from the safety kit: bandages in lots of sizes, tweezers for pulling out splinters and an instant cold pack.

After Neve and I each took a shower and got ready for bed, she disappeared for awhile. I got into my sleeping bag and tried to sleep. *Tomorrow is finally here!* I thought.

The soft rustling of cloth on the floor next to me made me open one eye.

Surprise, surprise. There was Neve, unrolling a sleeping bag. She slipped inside it and zipped it up.

"I guess I better get some practice with this sleeping-in-a-bag thing," she whispered as she plumped the pillow under her head.

Hmmmmm...maybe there was hope for Neve after all.

Chapter Three

HEIGH-HO! AWAY WE GO!

The next morning, Luckie woke us up bright and early. He was all paws climbing across our sleeping bags, with his tail wagging and swishing across Neve's face.

Luckie is a sweet old dog who mostly likes to snooze during the day. But when he's excited, he can be peppy*. He wanted to get started on our adventure.

We had a quick breakfast, brushed our teeth, packed our sleeping bags in the RV and jumped into the 4x4 car. Neve's stuffed animals and other belongings took up most of the legroom, but we made it work.

"Fasten your seat belts and buckle up for safety," said my mom. "You too, Luckie."

I adjusted Luckie's harness, which is a

seat belt made especially for dogs. Except for giving kisses and getting treats, there is nothing he likes more than going for a ride.

"Heigh-ho! Away we go!" my dad exclaimed as we pulled out of the driveway. "Now let's take a look at your maps and see what you've chosen as your special places to see."

Neve unfolded her map. I saw a ladybug sticker on Fresno, California. "Oh, I think our maps got mixed up, Neve. That's mine."

"I don't think so," said Neve. "Look, I wrote my name at the top."

I looked closer and saw that she was right. Her name *was* printed at the top. There was also an arrow that pointed to San Francisco and a heart that surrounded the words she'd written: "Home of Cynthia, my bestest best friend ever!"

I still didn't understand. I opened my map for her to see.

We were surprised to find that, out of the

entire United States, we'd both chosen a place to see in Fresno.

We were even more shocked* to discover that we'd chosen the *exact same place* in Fresno!

Neve explained the history of the underground home and gardens to my parents. "Over a hundred years ago, a man from Sicily bought farmland in California for growing fruit trees, but it turned out to be mostly rock. So what did he do? He started to dig. And he kept on digging—for 40 years!"

"He turned his huge mistake into something hugely magnificent," I added. "He built a beautiful home on three underground levels with tunnels, skylights*, bedrooms, a living room, kitchen, chapel and even his own fishpond!"

"And guess what?" Neve continued. "He made his dream of having a farm come true. He actually grew lemons, oranges, grapefruit and grapes underground."

My parents agreed that the tour of the underground gardens was a must-see.

"We can go to Fresno on the last day of our trip, right before we go to Neve's home in San Francisco," my mom said. "It will be a little tight, because Neve starts summer camp the day after that, but what a great way to end our trip!"

My mom took Backseat Fun envelope #1 from the basket and handed it to us.

Neve gave me a puzzled look as she pulled each item from the envelope. "A nickel? A deck of playing cards? A red pencil? A paper clip? String? A spoon? A bandana?" Then she smiled, holding up a book with the title *Easy and Amazing Magic Tricks*!

"Today you'll practice to become magicians," said my mom. "And there's one more thing inside."

"Look!" Neve exclaimed. She tipped the

envelope over and a rolled-up piece of paper fell on her lap. It was tied with a lemon-yellow ribbon. "It's our first Scavenger Hunt Clue!"

Scavenger Hunt Clue

Figure it out and find out where we're going tomorrow!

Native Americans called it "Thundering Waters" because this natural wonder roars! Make a wish when you see a giant rainbow over amazing falls and misty shores.

Hint: It's shaped like a "U."

"Loud water?" I asked.

"Misty shores?" asked Neve.

"Let's look at the map," I said. "That might help us patch together the clues."

We remembered the invisible trail my dad had drawn with his finger and I traced it with my finger. It went from the coast of Massachusetts across New York and through

Canada into Michigan.

"Maybe reading about those states in the travel guidebook will give us the answer," Neve said.

"It will go faster if we split it up," I suggested. "I'll read about Massachusetts while you read about New York."

A few hours later we saw a sign on the highway that said Seneca Falls, New York was just ahead.

"That's where the Women's Rights National Historical Park is," said Neve. She'd read an interesting book about it and explained it to me.

"About three hundred women and men met at the First Women's Rights Convention," she said. "They tried to figure out ways to make life better for women, including having the right to vote, own property* and get an education."

We all decided it would be interesting to

check it out. We toured sites around Seneca Falls such as the home of one of the organizers of the women's rights movement, Elizabeth Cady Stanton. We also saw the Wesleyan Chapel where the First Women's Rights Convention was held in 1848.

"Because of the convention, things slowly began to change," my mom told us. "But it wasn't until over 70 years later, in 1920, that women gained the right to vote."

It was hard to imagine that there was a time when women weren't allowed to vote.

We discussed that while we were having a picnic lunch. Afterwards, Neve helped me begin my travel journal. We jotted down notes about our stop in Seneca Falls and I decorated it with my first bumper sticker that said "Girls Rock!"

❧ ☙

Once we were back on the road, Neve and I asked my parents for hints about the clue. We made lots of guesses, but none of them were correct.

We decided to take a break from guessing and practice our magic tricks.

They had funny names like The Incredible Disappearing Pencil, The Wobbly Spoon and The Unstoppable Unpoppable Balloon.

The Button on a Tightrope trick involved balancing a red button on a piece of string. It made me think about the man who walked across a tightrope over Niagara Falls.

"My best friend Cynthia and I saw that on TV," said Neve. "The mist was so thick that it looked like the tightrope walker was in a rainstorm."

"Aha!" I exclaimed, with my pointer finger in the air. "Mist, loud water..."

"The answer to the clue!" Neve shouted, giving me a high five. "Niagara Falls!"

"Bingo," said my dad. "Tonight we'll stay at a campground that's not too far from the falls and tomorrow morning we'll tour them."

Late that afternoon, we arrived at the campground. While my dad went into the main office to pay for our campsite, Neve and I checked out the bulletin board on the side of the building.

It was covered by paper signs printed with all kinds of information. One explained campfire safety. Another was a map for hiking, with dotted lines that marked trails.

Neve excitedly tapped her finger on a bright yellow paper that said:

Calling all kids!
Please come, come, come and have fun, fun, fun
at the
Silly-Willy Olympics
Races today at 4:30 p.m.! Camp Activities Center

I could see Neve's lips moving, but I couldn't hear a word she was saying. Her voice was being drowned out by two girls in the parking lot who were singing at the top of their lungs like they were performing at a rock concert.

Neve and I glanced quickly at each other, then back at the kids.

The girl with beautiful long red hair and freckles was playing a guitar. The other girl also had red hair, but it was in pretty braids and she was playing a fiddle*.

Their lime-green car was painted with a winking and grinning sun face on the hood. The smile was a bit crooked, which gave it a goofy, happy look.

What's more, their old, really cool trailer was almost entirely covered with bumper stickers in all shapes and sizes. An amazing sight!

Not wanting to be impolite and stare, Neve and I both sort of awkwardly* turned around and continued looking at the yellow sign.

"My best friend Cynthia is the perfect three-legged race partner," Neve bragged. "If you're her partner, you're sure to win."

If she mentions her best friend one more time, I fumed*, *I think my head will explode!*

The rowdy* singing stopped, which made me curious. I slowly turned back around and was startled to see the singing girls right behind me. In fact, the guitar-playing girl was about two inches from my face. She stood with her arms crossed and her head tilted to one side.

"So," she said, "you think you can beat us?"

Chapter Four

COUSINS VS. SISTERS

The girl with the fiddle elbowed her sister. "Don't mind Kendra," she said. "She's just kidding around. Well, sort of. She always wins races."

She continued, hardly stopping for a breath. "I'm Kylie. This is Kendra. We're sisters."

Kylie kept speed talking, "That's my mom over there. Her name is Faith. And that's my dad, Ziggy, getting into our car. Our car is nicknamed Dusty and we call our little old trailer Rusty and—"

Kendra interrupted her, joking, "Rusty is so old he's *practically* held together by bumper stickers. We collect them from every place we travel. If it wasn't for bumper stickers, Rusty would probably fall apart!"

Suddenly, we heard Dusty's engine roar to life. The sisters hollered over their shoulders as they ran to the car. "See you at the Activities Center!" and "May the best sisters win!"

Their car doors slammed shut and Rusty began bobbling* along down the road behind Dusty, squeaking every time he hit a bump on the pavement.

"What was *that* all about?" Neve asked.

"I think they think we're sisters," I answered.

"I think they think we're going to let them win," Neve said.

"I think they're in for a big surprise," I replied.

I also *didn't* know what to think of these singing sisters with the zany* looking trailer.

உக்க உக்ல

Once we got to our campsite, we worked together to give it a "homey*" feel. We opened the canopy on the RV, unpacked the cooler and put a tablecloth on the picnic table.

We made a clothesline by tying a rope onto a tree to air-dry my heart-patterned towel, my ruffled pink-and-red bathing suit and Neve's striped bathing suit. Neve wanted to see what it was like to sleep in a tent, so my mom helped us pitch* our tent right beside the RV.

"Can we go to the Activities Center now?" I asked my parents, with my fingers crossed.

"Right after you both do 15 minutes of summer vacation reading for school," my mom said, as she handed us a timer.

"Pleeeeeeeease, Mom?" Neve and I were impatient to get to the Silly-Willy Olympics.

Sensing that the answer was not going to change, I got out a dictionary to look up any words we didn't know in our books. Neve and I sat down at the picnic table and set the timer for 15 minutes.

Suddenly, Neve jumped up off the bench. Swatting her hands around in the air, she looked like she was doing some kind of crazy dance. "A bee!" she shrieked. "I think I saw a bee!"

"That's a fly, not a bee," I said, and then scowled*.

"Oh that reminds me of a joke," my dad said, chuckling*. "You'll love this one. Why do bees hum?"

"Because they can't remember the words to songs," Neve and I chorused*.

I had to admit that joke was an oldie but a goodie.

The bell on the timer rang before I knew it. Neve and I laced up our sneakers and were off in a flash toward the Silly-Willy Olympics.

May the best cousins win, I thought.

There were lots of kids milling* around

the grassy park in front of the campground's Activities Center. We got there just in time for the three-legged race.

One of the camp counselors gave us a long piece of soft fabric that felt like a cut-up T-shirt. He told us to tie my right leg to Neve's left leg. The idea was to use two legs as if they were one leg.

As we were doing a few practice runs back and forth, Neve whispered in my ear. "There they are, those, those...*singing sisters*."

They were running up to the park and *still* singing. There was no guitar or fiddle, but it was the same song we'd heard earlier.

As soon as everyone was in a row at the starting line, a whistle blew to signal "GO!" Kids and parents on the sidelines were hooting and cheering.

Neve and I got off to a hilariously* rocky* start. I tripped, which made Neve fall. But we held onto each other and got back up. I could hear singing right behind us so I knew the sisters were at our heels*.

"Quick-quick!" I shouted to Neve.

"We can do it!" Neve panted.

It was close, but the judges declared us the champions of the Silly-Willy Three-Legged Race. There was much clapping and laughing at the finish line.

We each won a little kit with colored rope and instructions to make a friendship bracelet. The rope in Neve's package was my favorite color: bright pink. *Maybe Neve will trade with me*, I thought.

"Oh goodie!" Neve exclaimed, holding her package next to her heart. "I can't believe I got bright pink! That is my best friend Cynthia's favorite color. I'm going to make this friendship bracelet for her."

I snapped my mouth closed and turned away, just in time to see Kylie looking down at her digital watch which was beep-beep-beep-beep-beeping. She pushed a tiny red button on the side of the watch and said something to

Kendra that I couldn't hear. Kendra made a sour face.

More quickly than they'd run in the race, they dashed off in the direction of their campsite.

"Gee whiz! It's awfully competitive* to time yourself in a three-legged race," Neve said.

I swished my hand through the air as if pushing the sisters from my mind. "I guess that's the last we'll see of those sore losers."

Little did I know then just how wrong I was.

❧ ❧

That night I thought I heard sniffling coming from Neve's side of the tent.

"What's wrong, Neve?" I whispered in the dark.

"I think there's a rock under this tent and I'm lying right on top of it," she complained. "It feels like an oven in here. The tent is on a hill and all the blood is rushing to my head. I feel dizzy. Plus—"

"Neve," I said impatiently, "we put the tent on soft pine needles, remember? And you're on an air mattress, so how can you possibly feel a pebble?"

"The only good thing about camping," she said angrily, "is toasting marshmallows! And we didn't even do that tonight."

Why is she spoiling my good time? I wondered. *Why can't she just be happy?*

I heard another sniff. "Are you crying?"

"Must be my allergies," she mumbled*. "Maybe I'm allergic to camping."

Allergic to missing her parents was more like it. Allergic to Luckie's loving but slobbery kisses. Allergic to wishing she could be with her best friend who she keeps saying is "the coolest person ever."

It wasn't hard to figure out how Neve was feeling. No matter how much fun we'd had today, she was hundreds and hundreds of miles away from home tonight.

What can I do to take her mind off of

being homesick? I wondered.

As it turned out, I didn't have to do a thing.

The creepy, faraway howl of an animal was all it took to get our complete attention. OOOW-WUE! OOOW-WUE!

We sat bolt* upright in our sleeping bags and listened.

And then, a scratch-scratch-scratching noise made us shake with fear. I was positive that it was a big paw swiping across the top of the tent. We dove back into our sleeping bags and Neve huddled close to me.

Scra-a-a-a-a-a-atch, scra-a-a-a-a-a-atch. OOOW-WUE!

Chapter Five

LIONS & TIGERS & BEARS

Neve half-whispered, "What's that?! A mountain lion?! A tiger?!" Then she half-shouted, "A BEAR?!"

I tried to sound calm, although I was a bit scared myself. "Shh, shh, shh. Lions and tigers and bears don't live around here...well, maybe bears."

The next sound chilled me to the bone.

Z-z-z. Z-z-z. Z-z-z.

The zipper on the tent began slowly unzipping!

Now it was my turn to huddle closer to Neve. I held my breath. I didn't move a muscle. I squeezed my eyes shut, not wanting to see what dreadful, wild creature was about to have us for a midnight snack.

"Hello, girls," my dad said cheerfully as he poked his head in the tent. "Just checking to see if you're comfy in here."

The breath I'd been holding burst out.

Neve scrambled out of her sleeping bag. "May I please sleep in the RV, Uncle Marty?" she cried.

"Me, too?" I asked.

"Well, of course," he said. "You can try tenting some other night."

When I stepped out of the tent, I saw the "big scratching paw." It was a towel on the sagging clothesline. Swaying in the breeze, it brushed back and forth across the tent.

My mom was still sitting at the campfire. "I have a late-night craving for a s'more. How about you?"

We gladly took her up on the offer. Neve toasted her marshmallow just the way she likes it: lightly golden brown and only a bit warm on the inside. I cooked mine so it was perfectly burnt on the outside and so gooey on the inside it practically melted off the stick.

We sandwiched our marshmallows and chocolate between graham crackers.

I took a bite. "Yum," I said.

"So dee-lish," Neve said.

We might be complete opposites (well maybe not complete opposites), I admitted to myself, *but we both agree that toasting marshmallows is one of the best things about camping.*

A wonderful smell drifting through the screen on the RV window woke me up the next morning. I was amazed to find Neve with a spatula in her hand, flipping pancakes in a frying pan.

"Good morning, sleepyhead," my dad said to me as he petted Luckie.

"I made this one for you," joked Neve, as she handed me a plate. It was a big pancake shaped like a bear paw.

"Neve got up early to help with breakfast," my mom said, "so Shannon, you and I are on cleanup duty. Dad's chore is packing our lunches and water bottles in a cooler."

I knew from our pre-camping trip meeting what to do for cleanup duty. There was already a kettle on the campfire warming up water so we could wash and rinse the plates and camping cups. Then we'd put them on the rack to dry.

When everybody was done with their chores, we all hopped in the car, excited to see Niagara Falls.

"Heigh-ho! Away we go!" sang my dad.

Neve read some facts to us. "Niagara Falls is actually three falls. On the Canadian side is Horseshoe Falls, which is the largest of the three falls and is curved like a U. In the United States are the American Falls and the smaller Bridal Veil Falls."

We crossed the bridge from the United States into Canada and had a clear view of the falls, which are even more ginormous* than I'd imagined.

After we parked the 4x4 car, we walked on a long path that passed the falls and I took a gazillion pictures with my digital camera. It was a hot, sunny day and the cool mist from the falls felt as good as a sprinkler.

"Make a wish," I told Neve, pointing at a huge rainbow over the falls.

I made a wish that every day of our trip would be as fun as this one.

As we were driving along the highway in Ohio the following day, I quizzed my family

about the state.

"Did you know that 25 astronauts are from Ohio?" I asked. "Or that Thomas Edison was born in O—"

I was interrupted by a loud BEEP! BEEP! beside us. It was Dusty and Rusty cruising in the lane next to our car.

The sisters' parents both smiled and waved hello in their front seat. Kylie and Kendra appeared to be enthusiastically singing in the backseat. They were holding a handwritten sign up to the car window that said:

**Catch us if you can!
Ha!**

"They think we're racing," Neve said with a sigh. "They are so competitive."

Dusty and Rusty zoomed forward and into the lane in front of us. Rusty jiggled and wobbled from side to side.

"They'll be way ahead of us soon," I said hopefully, "so that's definitely the last we'll see of them."

Neve pointed at Rusty. "Not according to their license plate."

It read:

CYA L8R

I sounded it out and groaned.

Chapter Six

NEVER A DULL MOMENT

Even though driving across the United States means sitting for hours at a time, there was never a dull moment in our backseat.

Surprising things to see along the way (like a man riding a bicycle with a big parrot on his shoulder), games to play (finding cars with license plates from all of the states) and songs to sing (including the ones we made up) kept us entertained*.

In addition to the Scavenger Hunt and Backseat Fun Basket, we competed in Found It First! which is a game my mom made up. My dad and I were on one team and Neve and my mom were on the other.

Each team captain (Neve and I) got a list with 15 different items on it.

Whoever saw an object that was on either of

the lists shouted, "Found it first!" If the item was on your own team's list, you scored two points. If it was on the other team's list, you scored one point.

The team with the most points when we got to San Francisco would win.

Some of the items on the list were hard to find: a pink barn, a windmill, a man with a handlebar* mustache, a wishing well, a hot air balloon, five birds on a telephone wire and a weathervane that's shaped like an insect. You really had to keep your eyes peeled*.

Sometimes we'd create leaf rubbings by putting a sheet of paper over a leaf we'd collected. By moving the long side of a crayon back and forth over it, the colors of the crayons outlined the edges and veins of the leaves.

The leaf rubbings looked great in my travel journal along with the bumper stickers.

Usually, we'd begin driving in the morning and reach a campground in the afternoon. Sometimes we spent two nights at a campground so we'd have more time to see the sights.

After a long day of driving, Luckie always loved going for a hike with us. Neve warmed* up to hiking, too. We'd pack canteens* in our backpacks and a water bowl for Luckie. Then the five of us would explore trails through the woods, around ponds or up and down mountains.

Traveling with my cousin was like having a talking encyclopedia. She'd read enough books to fill a library and that's how she knew so many interesting things.

For example, she was reading a book about animal tracks. She showed me how you can often tell what animals have been on a path by looking for footprints in the earth.

The different shapes tell which tracks belong to what critter. We discovered raccoon, deer, wild turkey and skunk tracks, all on one path. That's a forest with a lot of traffic!

While I was on the lookout for four-leaf clovers, Neve was on the lookout for poison ivy plants (but we didn't find either!).

Neve also taught me about birds. I knew birds by ear, which is to say I could recognize many birds' songs and calls. It's like listening to a conversation in another language and figuring out what's being said.

Neve had read all about birds in science class, so she knew them by sight. The colors of their feathers, shapes of their beaks, and their sizes were all clues about their names.

We used our binoculars to get a closer look at who was making the beautiful music.

At dinnertime, we had Campfire Cook-offs*. Each team was responsible for making a dish, which was both fun *and* delicious.

Dad and I came up with Orange Ya Glad We Made Muffins (the muffin batter is cooked inside hollowed-out orange halves). Neve and my mom cooked Lickety-Split* Chili in a Can (yes, it's actually heated in a can over the fire!).

One winning recipe for the contest was Apple Pie Pockets. Neve and I dreamed it up one day while we were riding in the car.

We sliced apples, dotted them with butter, and added sprinkles of cinnamon and sugar. Then we "baked" them in tinfoil that we'd formed into sealed pockets.

Neve and I made a poster one day and when we got to our campsite we hung it on the RV door.

You're invited to a fireside show!
MAGIC UNDER THE STARS
Featuring the Backseat Magicians
When: Tonight
Where: Under the Big Dipper in campsite #13
What time: After dark
*Parents, dogs named Luckie
and fireflies are admitted for free.

Dressed in magician's capes (sheets) and pointed hats (made from black construction paper decorated with glitter), we directed our audience to their chairs (logs) by the campfire.

The "stage" was on the other side of the campfire in front of a picnic blanket hung on the clothesline (a perfect stage backdrop!).

Finally, it was showtime! The blazing campfire lit up our stage with a golden glow. Stars twinkled overhead. Smiling faces looked out from the "crowd."

Neve pretended to hold a microphone. "Ladies and gentlemen, dogs, fireflies and feathered friends! We are pleased to present our very first performance!"

I held up my magic wand (a twig) and exclaimed, "Let the magic begin!"

Neve and I took turns doing the tricks we'd been practicing in the backseat all the way from Massachusetts through New York, Ohio and Indiana, where we were camped that night.

My parents were wowed.

And judging by Luckie's face, he couldn't figure out how we did some of those tricks either. With his head tilted to the side, he stuck one ear up and folded the other down, as if to say, "*That* was amazing!"

After the show, Neve and I took a bow.

There was much applause, Luckie wagged his tail and smiled, and an owl hooted with approval.

"And now for my best trick, The Disappearing S'mores!" Neve joked as she stuck a marshmallow on her "magic wand" twig.

❧ ☙

A week after our trip began, disaster* struck for Neve.

We ran out of marshmallows.

The camp store was within view from our campsite, so my parents watched as Neve and I ran over to get a bag of marshmallows and a bumper sticker for my travel journal.

So far I had a bumper sticker from each place we'd visited, including a trail we hiked that Native Americans had traveled on long ago, a covered bridge (my mom's pick), a miniature* model of the United States Capitol that is made of wooden matchsticks and glue, and an insect museum (my dad's pick).

We knew who was inside the camp store before we even entered.

"It's those...those...*singing sisters*!" Neve said, shaking her head in disbelief.

Chapter Seven

THE MARSHMALLOW THIEVES

While Neve went to the store aisle where the marshmallows were kept, I spotted a wire rack at the cash register. It had just one bumper sticker on it. All the rest of the slots were empty.

Not much of a selection, I thought, *but at least there's one left*.

As I reached for the bumper sticker, someone else's fingertips plucked it from the rack.

Kendra's hand! The nerve!

If she noticed a look of anger on my face, she didn't show it.

"This will be the 250th bumper sticker we put on Rusty," she boasted. "One of the windows on the trailer has sort of been rattling, but this bumper sticker will fix that problem."

Kendra paid for the bumper sticker that would have looked so nice in my travel journal.

Neve stood behind her in line to buy marshmallows and a postcard to send to her parents.

Kylie frowned. "I wish *our* parents let *us* have marshmallows," she said to Neve.

"Yeah," said Kendra. "You're lucky."

The sisters looked at the bag of marshmallows, then at us, and then back at the bag.

"So…I think I saw your campsite," Kendra said, and then pointed, "is it right over there?"

"Yes," Neve said. "Where is yours?"

"It's on the other side of the circle," said Kylie. "Not too far from yours."

I thought I saw Kendra's eyes dart in the direction of the marshmallows again.

"Well, we'd better get going," I said, waving goodbye.

As we scooted quickly out of the store, Neve said quietly, "*Aaaawk*-ward!"

"Do you think they're going to stop by tonight when we're toasting marshmallows?" I asked.

"They might," Neve replied. "They know where our campsite is."

❧ ☙

The singing sisters did not stop by for

marshmallows that night...or so we thought.

However, when we unzipped the tent the next morning, we noticed the marshmallow bag right away. It was torn in three pieces on the ground. Every last marshmallow was gone.

The chocolate candy wrappers were shredded, and the chocolate had vanished. Not a single crumb was found in the graham cracker box.

Even the sticky ends of the toasting sticks were licked clean!

"Those, those...*stealing sisters*!" Neve cried.

Chapter Eight

'KNOT' WHAT YOU MIGHT EXPECT

It was my turn to open the Backseat Fun envelope later that morning. I dipped my hand inside and brought out two short ropes, two long ropes and the Backseat Knot Tying instructions.

Knot tying? I thought. *Seems sort of boring compared to some of the other fun things we've done, like learning the art of origami (which is folding squares of paper into birds, boxes and different shapes).*

I knew my mom had worked hard to put these envelopes together. I didn't want to hurt her feelings by having a bad attitude so I started reading the instructions out loud to Neve.

We practiced doing a simple knot that's perfect for hanging a clothesline between two trees so it doesn't sag (no more towels brushing against our tent and scaring us!).

We also learned how to make a sturdy knot that is just right for tying a canoe to a dock. We planned to go canoeing that afternoon so that knot would come in handy.

I joked with Neve, "I would *knot* have imagined that knot tying is so fun!"

"Well, I'm *knot* at all surprised," she joked back.

"It's really *knot* that hard, don't you think?" I asked.

"*Knot* if you follow the instructions," she said. And on and on it went with the knot jokes, until we were laughing like crazy.

The envelope also included another clue on a scrolled paper. Neve unrolled it and held it out for Luckie to study. "What do you think, fella? Where are we going?"

Luckie grinned and showed off his own teeth.

Scavenger Hunt Clue

*Figure it out and find out
where we're going tomorrow!*

Meet a 42-foot-long Tyrannosaurus Rex,
a dino who goes by the name of Sue.
Born 67 million years ago,
she used 58 knife-shaped teeth to chew.

*Hint: Her skeleton is in a famous museum.
Where is Sue now?*

He did not seem to have the answer, but he did have lots of wet, slobbery kisses for Neve. It surprised me when she laughed, hugged Luckie and told him that she loved him, too.

When we finally figured out the clue, we got excited to meet Sue! (See if you can figure out where she is. Then check at the back of the book for the answer.)

☙ ❧

Around the campfire that night we did a knot-tying demonstration for my mom, dad and Luckie.

Then we played Quiet Please! This game is played by doing nothing. If you think about it, doing nothing is doing something, but in this case doing nothing is being as silent as you can.

No wiggling around on the log you're sitting on. No scratching mosquito bites. No chewing bubble gum or snapping your fingers. Just listening. And then, when two minutes are up, we all say what we heard. Whoever heard the most sounds wins.

I heard a cricket chirping, a dog woofing, a snake slithering (*yes, really*) and a mosquito buzzing. Neve heard the fire crackling, an owl "whoo!", a hiccup, a trailer door slamming and a baby crying.

There was one thing that we *both* heard: two girls singing and playing the guitar and fiddle.

Those singing sisters! It seemed like we couldn't get away from them.

The next day, we passed a swimming test at the campground lake. The lifeguard at the beach gave us pink lifejackets and said we could use a canoe in a shallow*, roped-off area of the water.

There was another canoe already out in the water. And there was loud singing coming from it. The boat was rocking and making waves.

While we paddled around, I noticed my parents on the shore chatting with the sisters' parents.

Neve and I were practicing turns in our canoe when Kylie and Kendra challenged us to a race. We lined the canoes up together and decided where the "finish line" in the water would be.

It was probably the only time I've ever heard "On your mark, get set, go!" sung in harmony at a starting line.

The sisters were more into performing their song than paddling their canoe. Kylie pretended her paddle was a microphone. You would have thought the lake was surrounded by an audience. As she swayed from side to side, she dropped the paddle into the water.

Kendra reached over the edge of their canoe to get it, stretching her arm as far as she could. She scooched forward another inch, which caused her paddle to go overboard, too.

As we glided across the "finish line" we looked back at the girls. The rocking of their canoe had made the paddles drift away from them. The singing stopped. Without paddles, Kendra and Kylie were stranded. The canoe wasn't going anywhere.

Neve giggled which made me giggle. Kendra and Kylie pretended they didn't notice.

Since the water was only about knee-high, Kendra tried to jump out of their canoe so she could tow it to shore. That made the whole canoe tip over and both girls went splashing into the lake.

Besides getting soaked, the girls were fine. They easily turned the canoe over and collected their paddles.

"Serves them right for goofing off," Neve said under her breath.

"*And* for stealing our marshmallows," I added a little too loudly.

"What did you say?!" Kendra asked angrily. Her face was as red as an apple.

Before Neve could reply, Kylie's watch beeped. Kendra and Kylie hurried to pull the canoe up on the shore. They hopped quickly across the hot sand to their towels and dried off as they followed their parents down the dirt path to their campsite.

Chapter Nine

'X' MARKS THE SPOT

Later that week, as we were driving in the 4x4 car, my mom explained the mystery about why we kept running into Kendra and Kylie on our trip. The sisters' family was heading to a music festival in San Francisco. Our family was going to Neve's house which is also in San Francisco.

We were following the same path across the USA and camping in many of the same places.

"Oh no-o-o-o-o-o-o…," I groaned.

"Ziggy, Faith and the girls are a *really* nice family," my mom said, trying her best to convince us.

"But they're *really* bugging us, Mom," I complained.

"Did somebody say bugging?" said my dad. "That reminds me of a good joke. Why couldn't the butterfly go to the dance?"

"Because the dance was a *Moth* Ball!" Neve and I exclaimed at the same time.

"Guess what?" Neve said. "In less than a week we'll get to the underground gardens in Fresno, California! I'm so excited to see them!"

"Me, too!" I said.

"There's a lot to do and see before we get there, too," said my mom as she handed us a Backseat Fun envelope. It contained a Backseat Learn-to-Play-the-Harmonica Kit, with teeny-tiny harmonicas and instructions.

And it also held the next clue:

Scavenger Hunt Clue

Figure it out and find out where we're going today!

Check your map to discover where we'll travel next. You'll stand in four states at once on a circle marked with an "X."

Hint: It's the only place in the USA where four states touch each other.

This was a hard one! We looked over every inch of the map and finally found the only four states that touch each other (check out a map for yourself to find them, then look in the back of the book to see if your answer is correct).

That night, a Park Ranger stopped by our campsite to say hello and to remind us that hungry raccoons have been ransacking* campsites. Raccoons will steal whatever food is left out. They're *not* picky eaters.

He suggested putting our food in secure containers inside the RV at night. "Well folks, have yourselves a great night and remember to put your campfire out before you go to bed."

Neve and I looked at each other. We knew that we had made two mistakes: 1) leaving our ingredients for s'mores outside a few nights earlier, and 2) accusing Kendra and Kylie of stealing our marshmallows when it wasn't them at all.

Chapter Ten

BROKEN HITCH, FRIENDSHIP FIXED

We stopped at a picnic area by a stream a few days later.

"Fetch!" I called to Luckie as I threw a ball in a fenced-in area that was made just for dogs.

A scraping, squeaking noise got louder as it came closer to us. It was easy to recognize that it was coming from a colorful trailer named Rusty.

Once Dusty and Rusty came to a stop in the parking lot, Kylie, Kendra and their parents got out and bent over to look at the place where the trailer hooked onto the car. We joined them.

"The trailer hitch is broken," said Ziggy, as he wiped sweat from his forehead.

"I have a bumper sticker you could use," I suggested.

Even though I was trying to be helpful, all the parents seemed to think my offer was quite funny.

They talked it over and decided that the two moms would take my family's 4x4 car to get the part needed to fix the hitch.

However, the auto supply store was over an hour's drive away, so it was going to be a long, long wait at the picnic area with the singing sisters.

Neve, Luckie and I set off to explore the stream. Clear, cool water flowed around great big rocks that were perfect for climbing on. Kylie and Kendra played near us. Our dads sat together on the bank of the stream talking and watching us.

"I think we should say we're sorry for accusing them," Neve whispered to me.

We got up our nerve and blurted out an apology.

The girls actually laughed. "That's the first time we've ever been mistaken for raccoons!" Kylie said.

Pretty soon, there was a splashing contest, and then we all swam in a shallow pool made by a small waterfall. It was a blast.

We made up a game where one person dipped her finger into the water and drew a picture on a rock. Neve went first and drew an elephant. The rest of us had to guess what the picture was before the sun made the watermarks disappear.

Working together, we built a little dam* between two big boulders with branches and leaves and stones. Luckie must have thought we'd collected all the sticks for him, because he carried them one by one to my dad to play fetch with him.

Later, we looked for heart-shaped rocks for Neve's garden. She'll use them to create a border around her tomatoes, radishes and carrots.

After our picnic lunch, Kendra played her guitar and Kylie played her fiddle. They taught us how to play a simple song on them.

We discovered Kendra and Kylie were not only headed to a music festival in San Francisco, they were competing in the festival's talent contest called "You're a Superstar!" They said they'd been practicing their song for what seemed like a million years.

So that's what all the enthusiastic, loud singing was about!

We heard the now-familiar sound of Kylie's watch. She and Kendra explained that the alarm on her watch is set for 4:00 p.m. every day. It's their family rule that when the watch beeps, it's time to do their summer vacation reading for school. No ifs, ands or buts about it.

So Kendra and Kylie were not being overly competitive or sore losers at the three-legged race, I realized. *They were just disappointed that they had to go back to the campsite.*

84

Neve and I decided to sit under a shady tree with them and read our books, too.

❦ ❦

Later, we heard my mom call hello and saw her give the thumbs-up sign. "Mission accomplished! We have the new part for the hitch."

By working together, the parents fixed it quickly, and before long both families were pulling out of the parking lot and waving goodbye to each other.

"Heigh-ho! Away we go!" said my dad. "Our next stop is the largest natural bridge in the world, right here in Utah."

"Oh, wow! I saw Rainbow Bridge in the travel guidebook," I said. "It's made of rock, and it's almost as tall as the Statue of Liberty!"

"Are Kylie and Kendra going to the natural bridge, too?" I asked hopefully.

"No, they have other plans," said my mom.

Even though we were headed off for a new adventure, I felt a little sad that our afternoon was over. What started out as an awkward day "stuck" with the sisters had ended up to be one of our best vacation days yet.

Chapter Eleven

MORE MAGIC UNDER THE STARS

"I can't believe we saw a real dinosaur footprint at Rainbow Bridge on Tuesday!" I exclaimed as we settled in at another campground.

"Do you think it belonged to someone in Sue's family?" Neve joked as we unrolled our sleeping bags in the tent.

I plopped down on top of my sleeping bag. "I liked the replica* of the trading post we saw along the way, too."

Neve agreed. "It was interesting to see what kinds of things the pioneers could buy in those little stores."

Someone started humming nearby. Another hummer joined in, followed by the twang of a guitar and notes from a fiddle.

Neve hopped up. "It's the singing sisters! C'mon, let's go see them!"

We scrambled out of the tent to find Dusty and Rusty parked in the campsite right next to ours—and Kendra and Kylie performing on top of the picnic table!

That night there was a bright, full moon. Kendra, Kylie and their parents came to our campsite and we popped popcorn over the fire. We even saw a falling star.

Each of us talked about all the places we'd camped and compared stories. And we told the girls about the underground gardens we were going to see in Fresno.

"How does fruit grow underground?" Kylie asked.

"We'll send you a postcard and tell you how," Neve told them.

"Send us a bumper sticker from there, too," joked Kendra. "Rusty needs it. He has a loose screw on the door!"

Kendra went and got her guitar, Kylie brought her fiddle and Neve and I played our mini harmonicas. Our parents sang along.

Since we were almost to San Francisco, it was the last night we'd see our friends. They were leaving first thing in the morning so they could make it to the music festival in time for the talent contest.

Later, when Neve and I snuggled up in our sleeping bags, we agreed that the night had been fun. Fantastic. Magical.

"Let's get up in time to wish Kendra and Kylie good luck in the talent contest," Neve whispered.

"Good idea," I said as I drifted off to sleep. "We can count on all the noisy birds to wake us up early."

Either the birds were especially quiet that morning, or Neve and I were extra tired. We didn't hear the birds chirp or the sisters leave, and when we unzipped the tent, Dusty, Rusty and the whole family were already gone.

Neve and I were glum* and silent as we ate breakfast.

"C'mon now, girls," said my dad, "cheer up! We're finally going to see the underground gardens today!"

I *was* happy about seeing the gardens. Yet I felt tears welling up in my eyes. There was something else besides Kendra and Kylie leaving that was making me sad.

Neve. Today was my last day with her.

Tonight we would be bringing Neve to her house and staying overnight there. Tomorrow she was starting camp and we would be dropping off our rented 4x4 car and RV before heading to the airport to fly home.

My dream vacation—the one I'd planned for months and months—was coming to an end.

ॐ ॐ

I was sniffling, kneeling down and rolling up my sleeping bag when Neve peeked her head inside the tent.

"What's wrong, Shannon?" Neve asked.

"Must be my allergies," I said, trying to make a joke. "Maybe I'm allergic to the last day of camping."

"Me, too." Neve put her arm around my shoulder. "Listen, we have another problem right now."

"What are you talking about?" I asked.

"I think you'd better see for yourself," she said in a serious tone. She motioned for me to come with her out of the tent. When I did, she pointed at our RV.

"Neve, I don't know what you're trying to tell…" I stopped and stared.

There was Kendra's guitar case leaning against our camper! She'd accidentally left her guitar at our campsite last night. Without it, the sisters wouldn't be able to perform at the music festival that day. Neve and I had to make a decision—and quickly!

If we hit the road right away we could bring the guitar to Kendra and Kylie in time for the talent contest. BUT, that meant we would have to miss seeing the underground gardens. There wasn't time to do both.

Neve and I looked at each other, and then

at my parents.

"It's up to you two," said my mom.

"Yes," said my dad, "it's your choice."

Luckie stood by the guitar case. "Arf!"

We all laughed and started packing up the RV in a great big hurry!

Chapter Twelve

A CLUE FROM THE HEART

Throughout our trip, Neve and I had our hearts set on seeing the incredible underground gardens. But seeing our friends' dream come true was more important to us. And hearing them play up on the stage in front of all those people? It was amazing!

All of their practicing (on the hood of the car, in the three-legged race, in the canoe, at the picnic area, around the campfire) paid off. They won a 2nd place trophy, shaped like a big musical note.

❧ ❧

Luckie and Neve were leaning on each other and fast asleep as we drove along the last stretch of our trip to San Francisco.

It's funny, I thought, *making friends is a lot like following a map*. There are lots of twists and turns along the way.

I flipped through my travel journal and smiled. Neve and I had tons of fun the past three weeks. *Although we're opposites in some ways, we're alike in many ways, too*, I thought. And our differences actually made the trip more interesting.

After Neve left for camp the next morning, Luckie and I buckled up in the backseat and waved goodbye to Aunt Nellie and Uncle Bo.

I looked over at the left side of the backseat—"Neve's side" of the car.

Gone were the large, fluffy pillow, bag of snacks, lucky penny, extra-large picture of Cynthia, books, poison ivy cream, bug spray and her stuffed animals.

It looked so empty; except for a smallish, plain, brown paper bag on the seat.

I reached over, looked inside and found three things: the bright pink friendship bracelet she'd made, a rolled-up piece of paper and a "Welcome to San Francisco" postcard.

The postcard had a picture of an enormous orange bridge on it, which she'd drawn a heart around. And she'd written a note for me on the other side:

"Hi Shannon! You probably knew all

along that I was making this bracelet for you—I know pink is your favorite color! I hope you can figure out my clue. I already asked your mom and dad if it was OK and they said yes! XOXO, Neve ☺ "

I unrolled the paper and began reading:

Scavenger Hunt Clue

Figure it out and find out
where we're going <u>next year</u>!

You've always been my cousin,
but now you're my true friend.
That's why I figured out a plan
so our travels together won't end.

Meet me where the backseat is windy,
the dog kisses are wet,
and the glittering lights of the bridge
start our "next" best adventure yet.

Hint: A ♥ *marks the spot.*

Glossary

Many words have more than one meaning. Here are the definitions of words marked with this symbol * (an asterisk) as they are used in sentences.

4x4, as in "4x4 car": *a vehicle that can be driven on paved or unpaved roads*
awkwardly: *uncomfortably*
bobbling: *moving in a bouncing way, up and down and side to side*
bolt, as in "bolt upright": *sitting with a straight back*
canteens: *small water bottles for camping*
chorused: *said the same thing at the same time*
chuckling: *laughing quietly*
competitive: *wanting to be better at something than others*
cook-offs: *contests to see who cooks the best*
cross-country: *from one side of the country to the other*
destination: *the place you are going to*

dam: *a wall built to hold back water*

disaster: *an event that causes much damage*

entertained: *amused and interested*

fiddle: *violin*

fumed: *thought angrily*

ginormous: *enormous*

glanced: *looked quickly*

glum: *sad*

handlebar, as in "handlebar mustache": *a mustache that is wide and thick, with ends that curve up*

heels, as in "at our heels": *close behind*

hilariously: *very funny*

homey: *comfy, cozy*

lickety-split: *quick*

milling: *gathering and moving in circles*

miniature: *a very small copy of something that is usually bigger*

mumbled: *said quietly and not clearly*

muttered: *spoke in a low voice or grumbled*

peeled, as in "keep your eyes peeled": *watch carefully*

peppy: *full of energy*

pitch: *set up*

property: *a thing that belongs to someone*

punch line: *the last part of a joke that makes it funny*

ransacking: *searching a place and stealing things*

replica: *a model of something*

rocky: *difficult*

rowdy: *noisy*

scowled: *looked irritated*

shallow: *not deep*

shocked: *surprised*

skylights: *openings or windows in a ceiling*

squabbling: *arguing noisily*

stewed: *worried*

warmed, as in "warmed up to": *began to like*

zany: *unusual in a funny way*

Lucky 13!

Did you know that this is the 13th book in the Our Generation®
Book Series? We call that lucky! That's why we put
13 luck-related words, numbers and phrases in the story.
Can you find all 13 listed below?

• Rainbow • Fingers Crossed • 7 • Horseshoe• 13
• Good Luck • Lucky Penny• Falling Star • Elephant
• Wishing Well • Luckie • Four-Leaf Clover • Ladybug

Turn a road trip into a fun scavenger hunt!

Here's how Shannon and Neve played Found It First!:

1. Use two players or two teams. Make copies of the lists on the next two pages to share. There's a different list of objects to find for each player/team.

2. When you see an object that's on either of the lists, shout "Found it first!" If the object is on your own list (or your team's list), you score two points. If it's on the other player's list (or the other team's list), you score one point. Once an object is found, it gets crossed off the list and can't be found by the other team.

3. The team with the most points by the time you get to where you're going wins!

Found It First!
Scavenger Hunt #1

1. a cloud that looks like a giraffe
2. a pink barn
3. a car pulling a racecar
4. a round bumper sticker
5. a cornfield
6. an ambulance
7. a billboard with a doughnut on it
8. a moving train
9. a person wearing a bright yellow vest
10. an antique (really really old) car
11. a windmill
12. a man with a handlebar mustache
13. a wishing well
14. a hot air balloon
15. five birds on a telephone wire

Found It First!
Scavenger Hunt #2

1. a cloud that looks like a duck

2. a purple barn

3. a car pulling a speedboat

4. a funny bumper sticker

5. an apple orchard

6. a helicopter

7. a "Baby on Board" car window sign

8. a four-leaf clover

9. a pink car

10. a weathervane shaped like an insect

11. a bow tie

12. a fancy hat

13. an American flag on a pole

14. a statue

15. a license plate that spells a word

Answers to Scavenger Hunt Clues in the Book

Chapter Eight: Sue's skeleton is displayed at the Field Museum in Chicago, Illinois. She had very long teeth—up to one foot long!

Chapter Nine: Four Corners Monument marks the only spot in the USA where four states meet: Arizona, Colorado, New Mexico and Utah.

Chapter Twelve: Where will Shannon and Neve begin their next trip? At the Golden Gate Bridge in San Francisco, California.

this is **our** story

We are an extraordinary generation of girls. And have we got a story to tell.

Our Generation is unlike any that has come before. We're helping our families learn to recycle, holding bake sales to support charities, even holding penny drives to build homes for orphaned children in Haiti. We're helping our little sisters learn to read and even making sure the new kid at school has a place to sit in the cafeteria.

All that and we still find time to play hopscotch and hockey. To climb trees, do cartwheels all the way down the block and laugh with our friends until milk comes out of our noses. You know, to be kids.

Will we have a big impact on the world? We already have. What's ahead for us? What's ahead for the world? We have no idea. We're too busy grabbing and holding on to the joy that is today.

Yep. This is our time. This is our story.

www.ogdolls.com

Power of a Girl Initiative

For every Our Generation doll, outfit or accessory you buy, 10¢ goes to Free The Children's Power of a Girl Initiative to help provide girls in developing countries an education—the most powerful tool in the world for escaping poverty.

Did you know that out of the millions of children who aren't in school, 70% of them are girls? In developing communities around the world, many girls can't go to school. Usually it's because there's no school available or because their responsibilities to family (farming, earning an income, walking hours each day for water) prevent it.

Free The Children has now built more than 650 schools which educate more than 55,000 children throughout the developing world. Free The Children also builds and fosters sustainable villages through healthcare, water programs and alternate income projects for moms and dads that give girls the opportunity to get the education they need.

The most incredible part is that most of Free The Children's funding comes from kids just like you, holding lemonade stands, bake sales, penny drives, walkathons and more.

Just by buying an Our Generation doll or accessory you have helped change the world, and you are powerful (beyond belief!) to help even more.

If you want to find out more, visit:
www.freethechildren.com/girls

FREE THE CHILDREN
children helping children through education

Free The Children provided the factual information pertaining to their organization. Free The Children is a 501c3 organization.

About the Author

Susan Cappadonia Love lives in Milton, Massachusetts with her husband, Scott and daughters, Sophie and Olivia. They provided the imagination for many of the ideas in this story.

In addition to **Magic Under the Stars**, she has also written eight other books in the Our Generation® Series, **The Circus and the Secret Code, The Most Fantabulous Pajama Party Ever, The Jukebox Babysitters, The Dress in the Window, The Sweet Shoppe Mystery, The Mystery of the Vanishing Coin, Stars in Your Eyes** and **One Smart Cookie**, as well as other children's books.

This story came to life because of all the wonderful people who contributed their creativity and vision, including Joe Battat, Dany Battat, Alison Morin, Batia Tarrab, Natalie Cohen, Loredana Ramacieri, Karen Erlichman, Lisa Skolnick, Gillian Greenberg, Sandy Jacinto, Joanne Burke Casey and Pam Shrimpton.

this is my vacation story:

_____

_____

_____

_____

_____

_____

_____

_____

_____

_____

_____